THE BROONIE

AND OTHER DARK POEMS

DEBORAH SHELDON

The Broonie and Other Dark Poems

Deborah Sheldon

All rights reserved. No part of this book may be reproduced or transmitted in any form or by any means, electronic or mechanical, including photocopying or recording or by any information storage and retrieval systems, without expressed written consent of the author and/or artists.

The Broonie and Other Dark Poems is a work of fiction. Names, characters, places, and incidents are products of the author's imagination. Any resemblance to actual events or persons, living or dead, is entirely coincidental.

Poem copyrights owned by Deborah Sheldon
Cover illustration by James @ GoOnWrite.com
Overall cover design by Marcia A. Borell

First Printing April 2025

Hiraeth Publishing
P.O. Box 1248
Alamogordo, NM 88310
e-mail: hiraethsubs@yahoo.com

Visit www.hiraethsffh.com for online science fiction, fantasy, horror, scifaiku, and more. Stop by our online Shop for novels, magazines, anthologies, and collections. **Support the small, independent press…and your First Amendment rights.**

For Allen

Table of Contents

7	*Introduction*
9	The Broonie
10	Flamingo-Pink Balloon
12	408 Kilometres Up
13	Amazon Warrior
17	First and Last Foray
19	The Sea Will Have
20	Witchcraft Doll
21	Ancient Cogs Beneath
22	The Midwife
25	Into My Parlour
26	Sarah Joins the Circus
29	Parasitic Births
30	Smothered, Still and Silent
31	Frantic Flight, Rising, Rising
32	Galérien
34	On the Cusp
35	An Unusual Request
36	The Door
37	The Coach from Castlemaine
42	Wheals and Whorls
43	*Afterword*
48	*First Publication Credits*
49	*Author Biography*

Introduction

Throughout my long and varied career, I've tackled almost every medium of writing that interests me, including magazine articles, TV scripts, medical writing, non-fiction books, plays, short stories, novellas, and novels. Part of my enjoyment is learning about and respecting each medium's principles and parameters. Over the years, I've found that mediums tend to overlap, sharing at least a few transferable skillsets. For example, if you can already write a TV script then writing a stage play isn't too much of a stretch.

Poetry, however, is a tricky beast that sits apart on its own island.

Consider this: prose has relatively few limits, and you're free to construct a sentence in whichever way you like. Conversely, writing a story using a poetic form impels you to construct a puzzle with no missing or leftover pieces. Each form has its own strict rules about the exact number of lines, syllables, stanzas, rhymes and refrains, to list just some of the possible constraints.

The central question is: *How do I figure out this puzzle?*

For me, the bridge is cryptic crosswords. I'm passionate about them. The area of my brain that loves to solve cryptic crosswords lights up whenever I'm writing poetry. Both activities present an intriguing challenge.

Another passion of mine is adaptation. Such as reworking my published short stories into plays; an optioned screenplay into a published novel; a novella into a screenplay. It's about the riddle of figuring out how to reshape my own plot, characters, atmosphere and theme into a new format. If I'm to find the heartbeat that would resonate the best, the story's essence must first be laid bare. I have to cut the story open, expose its backbone and innards, put each piece under a microscope, pick and choose, be mindful of where I put my stitches. The difficulty of having to abide by another medium's rules allows me to scratch my puzzle-solving itch.

Which explains how this collection came about.

Each poem is my deep dive into a specific poetic form, as well as my rendition of a drabble, flash fiction piece, or short story of mine that's already been published.

For instance, my award-nominated poem "The Broonie" is a brisk interpretation of my story "*Post Hoc Ergo Propter Hoc*", which previously I had adapted into a prize-winning stage play. To tell this horror tale as a poem, I chose the villanelle. This poetic form is so notoriously difficult to write that it's known amongst poets as 'exquisite torture'. I concur! The demands of the form insisted that I strip away and excise almost everything from the story until what I had left was the tortured nub of my character's state of mind. The process felt exhilarating.

Most of the poems herein are original to the collection. "The Sea Will Have", my first published poem, was released in 2020 and I've written many poems since then, all of a darkly-speculative nature. Some have been published in various anthologies and magazines including *Illumen*, of which Tyree Campbell is the editor. My heartfelt thanks go to Hiraeth Publishing and Tyree, its managing editor, for releasing my first collection of poetry.

I hope you enjoy it.

Deborah Sheldon
Melbourne, Australia, 2025

The Broonie

Scritch, the scratching wakes me, I hear the creep
of the broonie living inside our walls.
I swallow pills and booze to make me sleep.

Hired exterminators can't hear a peep,
the companies have stopped taking my calls.
Scritch, the scratching wakes me, I hear the creep.

I bash out plaster, wood, tiles, wade knee-deep
in detritus; in search I've wrecked our halls.
I swallow pills and booze to make me sleep.

Broonie always haunts, causes me to weep,
yet doctor mocks, offers drugs and catchalls.
Scritch, the scratching wakes me, I hear the creep.

Will broonie sneak by beds in silent sweep?
His claws rip our hair, slash our scalps, our skulls?
I swallow pills and booze to make me sleep.

I'm tired of fear, of life, give me the deep
instead of harking breathless to footfalls.
Scritch, the scratching wakes me, I hear the creep—
I swallow pills and booze to make me sleep.

Flamingo-Pink Balloon

The man in the neighbouring hospital bed
snored as if he were screaming; a constant *argh
argh*. Elsie cursed him, and wished for her homestead
but her hip wouldn't heal, the prognosis vague.
Day after day, she endured *argh argh*, and then
one morning, he sat up and bellowed, "You rogue!
I'm at my end, blast you. Take the old grey hen,"
and fell back. Nurses wheeled his bed to the morgue.

Alone, relieved, Elsie watched out the window.
Across the courtyard, behind another pane
bobbed a balloon, as pink as a flamingo.
To mark a birthday, perhaps, with banned champagne
camouflaged in thermos flasks. There would be cake…
She felt a fervent wish for a visitor,
but she was old, kith and kin dead. Sharp heartache
momentarily held Elsie prisoner.

She pushed aside loneliness from long habit,
stiffened her spine, chose to look forward to lunch,
when something struck the window sill and grabbed it
with bony hands. Elsie's insides seemed to bunch
in sudden fear. Somehow it was the balloon,
bright flamingo pink, that bobbed at her window,
set with features dark like the man on the moon,
its skeletal fingers tapping. A limbo

within which she understood the snoring man's
final words had been addressed to this creature,
his curse was to include Elsie in his plans.
She was the "old grey hen", of that she was sure
as she gazed into each black, bruised eye socket
of this balloon-headed monster. *Tap, tap, tap*
on glass. Soon, it would find a gap, a pocket
somewhere in the sill, float across the room, trap

10

her in its suffocation. Elsie, gasping,
looked away, glanced up at the dead TV screen
high above her bed, screwed into the ceiling,
and saw the reflection of its jaunty lean,
its spidery limbs, its giant head so close,
near enough to kiss. Yelping, she looked around
at nothing, an empty room. "Nurse, please, a dose!"
she cried. (Surgery must have had a profound

effect on Elsie's anxious state of mind.)
Drugged, she kept her eyes shut. Allowed dusk to creep
around the closed slats of the room's window blind.
At long last, Elsie felt brave enough to peep.
In the TV reflection, the monster leered.
Elsie knew she was doomed, realised with unease
that her life, by this ghoul, had been commandeered.
She called for help, but *argh* was all she could wheeze.

408 Kilometres Up

The Earth whips by through lone porthole,
A bluish beachball, nothing more.
To crash this station is my goal.

Alone in orbit, such a bore.
For months! They lied, had told me days.
A bluish beachball, nothing more.

"An average man", to paraphrase,
Hand-picked because I'm fat and slow.
For months! They lied, had told me days.

Our radio long gone – good-oh!
All rations done; air full of shit.
Hand-picked because I'm fat and slow.

The other volunteer? King-hit.
Dead, of course. How to share pent space?
All rations done; air full of shit.

He bobs around, I watch his face
The Earth whips by through lone porthole.
Dead, of course. How to share pent space?
To crash this station is my goal.

Amazon Warrior

Philantha sees the horses first,
beneath a tree, penned by branches.
No one about. She advances,
warily, ignoring her thirst,
her hunger, the wound she has nursed
since the doomed battle to save Troy;
her arm cut by a Greek, a boy.
She repaid his sword with her spear
and ran him through, twice, stole his gear
and fled. She is without convoy.

A hot cloudless sky bakes the plain.
Her feet crunch dead meadow flowers.
Nervous horses snort. One cowers
from her hand. She sings, pats his mane,
he calms. Oh, their Trojan campaign
was for naught; she'll ride home at speed
to Thermiskyra on this steed.
From the grasses, a man sits up.
Shackled, naked, dirty; a pup
that poses no threat. "Hah! Take heed!"

He says, "Go, and flee while you can
before my mistresses come back.
You're an Amazon! They'll attack
and kill you outright. Your daft plan
of horse-stealing is dafter than
your allegiance to King Priam.
Woman, how could you be so dumb?"
Philantha surveys the man's chain,
says "I'll free you, then leave this plain."
He points, laughs. "Too late! You'll succumb."

She looks to the dirt road nearby—
no one. She listens, hears nothing.

She'll open the corral and spring
upon this horse, which does not shy
from her touch. Then she looks up high
into the tree. Its leaves are fouled
with shit, as if birds have crowded
the branches. The tree holds no birds.
The man laughs, "Can't you see their turds?"
Shapes are silhouetted by cloud.

Shapes of bulky birds, advancing,
big as vultures, but these are worse.
Harpies. Philantha breathes a curse
as the hag-birds approach, winging
to land, Philantha's wound stinging,
and her only weapon a spear.
"You shouldn't have been cavalier,"
mocks the man. Both harpies touch down,
awkwardly, like bats, totter, frown
at Philantha with a cold sneer.

Breasts, arms, typical of woman,
each face as white as a flayed skull,
puckered eyes blinking dank and dull,
lipless mouths flexing, inhuman.
The man snickers, "Look what you've done,
Amazon, secured your demise.
Anyone trying to fight – dies."
Philantha lifts her spear, presses
her toes in the dirt, muscles flex
for the onslaught. She moves crabwise.

"Girl, I'm Odarg," says the big one,
"You need to make peace with your gods."
Philantha says, "You lack the odds,
you are two, but you'll both be gone."
"Kill her now!" shouts the man, "have fun
with her corpse, then chomp on her guts."
The small harpy says, "No smugness!

Call a truce. She might be wounded,
but take care! I have concluded
that she'll slay us all with quick cuts."

Odarg snarls, "Drop spear, Amazon."
She replies, "Come take it from me,"
but she's backing close to the tree.
The Amazon looks weak and wan—
This battle is already won.
Hah! Odarg smiles at her sister.
"We'll give the dregs to your mister,"
she remarks while she shows her nails,
each claw poisoned as the folktales
describe. "No one to assist her."

Convinced, the little one snarls, leaps.
Quick, strong, Philantha lifts the spear,
which cleaves through to the stringy rear
of the small harpy. Dark blood seeps
into the dry soil. Odarg weeps.
"Take the horse," Odarg cries, "and flee,
but somewhere on the road there'll be
a host of us waiting for you.
We'll smash and bash you, black and blue.
Rue the day you walked to my tree."

Weak, ill, Philantha mounts the horse
and trots from the meadow, leaving
there a harpy and man wailing,
their grief fresh. Philantha, of course,
knows the harpies will chase in force.
Will infection kill her instead?
Faint, she lets the horse have its head.
Trotting north-east, towards her home,
the hooves clip-clop like metronome.
Philantha frets in darkest dread.

The harpies will advance like owls.
Soft and quiet, with sharp talons drawn,
they'll assail by night or by dawn.
Philantha knows this in her bowels.
Her horse is tired, and evil prowls
about her as the sunset gloams.
She steels herself by seeing homes
in her mind's eye: there, the Black Sea
with boats working nets by the quay
and, by the shore, the catacombs.

First and Last Foray

Friday evening, lights high,
hopes higher in this pub
full of old rejects like me, a divorcée,
shamming to the hubbub.
I check my watch, the door,
feigning a tardy date,
masking from strangers my fear of their judgement
while flaunting myself: bait.

If no man approaches
I'll huff, pay my tab, leave—
God, I'm such a fool playing this role. I squirm,
hating this make-believe,
yet the miracle hits.
Red wine is bought for me!
By whom? Bartender won't say. If I accept?
That suggests I agree.

Married for years, I'm scared,
I don't know what to do.
The bartender says, "Hon, you only live once."
I sip, to follow through.
The man who approaches
is fat with a hard face—
I'm no prize anymore either; gone, the girl
that men once loved to chase.

If you live long enough
you get to lose it all,
bit by awful bit, until at last, nothing.
I'm fighting this downfall.
Which is why I say, "Yes!
Let's go and see that band!"
Then I leave with him, this hard-faced, fat stranger
just to spite my husband...

My ex, who doesn't care,
too busy screwing *her*.
I gloat revenge as we stroll next door to
the bar. Too soon it's a blur,
this second location,
as live rock thumps loud,
and after one drink, I'm left spinning. Spinning.
I need to leave this crowd—

Waking up in a car,
groggy, sights flashing by,
the fat man driving. My legs numb, head pounding,
I whisper, "Where am I?"
The car slows and pulls up
at a house with a spire.
Too late. I'm weak, can't run. And now—I'm just an
object of his desire.

The Sea Will Have

North Sea, calm and green, an English meadow
Lifts the ship on gentle swells, storm long gone.
For cod, sprat and herring, the deck hands throw
The trawling nets on their last bloody dawn.
North Sea, flat and harmless, bath for a child
Voices a note that sings through the marrow.
The men lose their heads, blood-quickened and wild,
Visions of women, sea nymphs Calypso.
The crew cannot swim but leaps overboard,
And each mate is held in unyielding grip.
The women are gilled, and some of the horde
Slice through the nets to free fish from the ship.
Dragged to the seabed, the drowning souls pray;
Unanchored, unmanned, the ship drifts away.

Witchcraft Doll

Wooden sticks
bound with twine
make an x,
make you mine.

Beads for your
mouth, nose, eyes.
Cloth and glue,
knots, kinks, ties.

Now the wax.
Candle lit
drip, drip, drip
along slit,

belly, breasts.
My voodoo
will bind us.
I love you.

Ancient Cogs Beneath

Sun-drenched beach, caster-sugar sand
And tourists swim, kids at play,
Play; fun and laughter, joyful noise—
Noise of scraping floods the bay.

The bay gapes holes deep in the strand,
And people scream, drop straight down,
Down, swallowed by the rumbling grains
Grains that cover, smother, drown.

"Drown? I'll take my chances," says one,
One girl, who flees to water.
Water begins to shiver, whirl...
Whirl. Then the vortex caught her.

The Midwife

A village on Lord Ralf's estate was hemmed by woodlands dark
That were known to harbour wolves and bears and more.
If you ventured too far in, entranced by branches, leaves and bark
You'd be lost to lurking creatures, said folklore.

In the meadow by this wood, a new wife foraged for her pot
To bulk her husband's evening meal with herbs and shoots.
Again, Joan was with child, her others sloughed, and left to rot
In the ground, just cast aside, and trod by boots.

Peeping through the oaks arose a soft and pallid light,
Which was small, as round as cheese, a sight so pure.
And as she turned towards it, sad heart lifting, gay and bright,
Many more swooped down to join the dancing lure.

Joan forgot about her basket, spellbound, wandered in a daze,
And prepared to slip by trunks and lose her way,
When the cramping hit her, made her fall, the pain set
     mind ablaze.
God, her waters broke – her babe would birth this day.

She cried for husband, "Gilbert!", who was chocking roof
     with thatch,
And he flung aside his tools, raced to her side.
He carried her to home and fastened tight the safety catch
On the door, but let the midwife come inside.

The labour long and hard, the couple feared another death
Yet the midwife said good harvest was a sign.
And when Adam lay on straw – their son! – and took first
     vital breath,
His little life was proof of God's design.

"We'll baptise him on Sunday," Gilbert said, "as it's the way."

But the midwife, old and wizened, shook her head.
"Your blue-eyed son is blonde, and will attract the monsters fey,
"If you don't protect him now, he's good as dead.

"For the faeries will replace him with a spell of sticks and dirt
To repay their tithe to Hell of someone's child,
And they won't give up their own, which is why yours will be hurt,
You should hold him close to chest." But Gilbert smiled.

"We spurn your superstition, God is watching overall,"
He scolded, as he packed a bag to go.
"I'm off with dozen men to buy some oxen with our haul
The village harvest means we have some cash to throw."

Poor Joan begged him to stay, recounted tale of woodland lights
Yet her husband shrugged it off with careless frown,
She was left alone with Adam, freshly born – yet what of sprites
That were watching from the woodlands, close around?

Each light a twist of straw, the midwife told, and set ablaze
A burning fire like torches marching in the night.
The candles lit which pull the unaware through deadly maze
Forced to drown in boggy marsh or die from fright.

Without her husband, Joan did try to do her daily chores,
Tend the vegetables, and goats and chickens too,
Yet her son refused the breast, and seemed to hate
 the world outdoors
And would lay there boneless, sickly, tinged with blue.

The midwife felt his limbs and gave her verdict: "Not a child!"
In fact, he was a changeling, made of sticks.
"If you throw him in the fire," she said, "the changeling
 so beguiled
Will be forced to cede its evil bag of tricks.

"Girl, trust me," urged the midwife, as she moved
 towards the hearth

"If you burn your changeling, faeries will return,
"And bring your child to you, but he'll be foul, just give him bath.
"Believe me, put aside naive concern."

Joan held her baby fast and placed a kiss upon his brow
When he opened up his eyes to meet her gaze.
"He's my child," she said, and wept as midwife gave a subtle bow
And answered, "If you want a fake, yes, with malaise!

"But if you want your Adam, put this mannequin of lies
In the flames; and make the faeries give your boy."
So, Joan in tears, without a choice, she had to exorcise
This wily changeling, which she let the flames destroy.

Into My Parlour

"Give me your palm, sir, and I'll read your fate,"
I crooned. My chump's flashing eyes warned of strife.
"Mother was swindled," he snarled, "took your bait."
Out from his jacket he brought forth a knife—
"Give back her money or I'll take your life."
I smiled, then laughed, which incensed him no end.
"You charlatan!" Yes, what need to pretend?
He leapt up, "You'll die!" Then I pulled a gun.
My chump dropped the knife, begged hard to amend.
Forget it, I win! I'm never outdone.

Sarah Joins the Circus

Torn from orphanage when she was ten.
"Those nuns you will never see again,"
said the men in Sarah's new family:
a dad, two sons. "Mum" bothered now and then.

They are all red-haired, freckled and pale.
Olive-skinned Sarah has eyes of shale
which they rail against. *Sarah is beastly.*
The nuns lied. They promised a fairy tale—

Of hugs, toys, kisses, trips to the zoo,
birthday cakes, picnics, relatives too;
none ever came true. Sarah puzzles, "Why me?"
Why choose her – whom they despise – to rescue?

One day she'll find her *real* mum and dad,
Seen at a circus years' back, full-clad
in leotards as they'd worked the trapeze—
"Stop it," the nuns said. "You'll drive yourself mad."

In the ring, a dachshund, trembling
sat on a tricycle, trundling,
whimpering as the crowd laughed with such glee—
Sarah dreams of that stunt: cruel and haunting.

It is her birthday but Sunday too.
That means the aunt with children is due.
The children run through their insults with glee—
"You're not one of us." "Your real ma hates you."

When raining, they mock Sarah indoors.
When sunny, they mock Sarah outdoors.
Push, kick her down on all fours; she won't flee
or fight back. To do so would cause uproars.

"Your birthday?" Aunt says at lunch and smiles,
"Want a gift?" Sarah's used to Aunt's guiles
and the cousins' wiles, but... "Something for me?"
Sarah whispers. A respite? No more trials?

Aunt stands, lifts from the clotheshorse nearby
a wire coat-hanger meant for drip-dry
and gives it, thereby, to her addressee:
Sarah. All at the table laugh. *Bull's eye!*

They've done it at last, brought out the tears
that Sarah's clenched tight inside for years.
As her ears ring with their joyful *esprit*
she thinks of the circus dachshund, the jeers...

The lights white hot, the dog shaking, scared,
crying for comfort – nobody cared.
Sarah, shoulders squared, can set herself free
for she holds the hook and no one's prepared.

She leaps from the chair and takes a swipe.
Coat-hanger slices through cheek so ripe—
she missed his windpipe. Cousin is lucky!
Gore shines red, high screaming, his lips blue tripe.

Now, Sarah is part of the circus,
the monkeys are hooting and clueless.
She makes a mess, rips out teeth, *one two three!*
Ruptures eyeballs, lips and noses. Success!

The swinging hook is a wee trapeze.
Her circus blood drives all to their knees.
They beg, "Please", but nuh-uh, Sarah with glee
shall go on and on, until she's at ease.

And when she's done, the doorbell will ding.
The nuns on the step will say, "Poor thing,
come home to the circus ring, and you'll see
both parents – you're high-wire artists' offspring."

Parasitic Births

The pain bites deep, an endless flood
from stricken womb, a stream of blood.
Not menopause, no, couldn't be,
it's monsters that she cannot see
with hair and teeth, they rend and scud.

Pronouncement – *fibroids* – growths that bud
through walls of wombs like weeds in mud.
The answer – *hysterectomy*.
The pain bites deep.

A surgeon's paid to purge the crud—
he'll let them loose instead. Dear God!
The bastard wants them roaming free
to chew through liver, bowel, kidney,
and this he does; he splits the pod.
The pain bites deep.

Smothered, Still and Silent

Floodwaters lap at my house all night long,
Sopping, sighing. Electricity out,
Home so quiet. Morning brings no birdsong
And I open the curtains, look about,
See no sign of water. Instead: whiteout.
Snow across my property, trees and lawn.
Snow in autumn? How? Shocked, I want to shout.
Utter silence. The world's noises are gone.

No barking dogs, no trill of currawong,
No sound of neighbours. I begin to doubt...
Snow? I lift the window and flinch. Strong,
Musky stink – sweet, sick and rancid – has clout.
Wait! There, floating on the breeze, a great rout
Of spiders in their millions, threads airborne.
"Snow" is webs; landed after the washout.
Utter silence. The world's noises are gone.

Panicked, I drive from the garage. If wrong,
Then fleeing my house does nothing but out
Me as a coward. So what? Through the throng
Of webs I force my car, taking the route
To town. Clogged roads as far as I can scout.
Kerbside, cocooned vehicles. This white dawn
Is death. Spiders breach my car. Webs sprout.
Utter silence. The world's noises are gone.

I try to pray; I've never been devout.
Spiders spin mesh around my head, stick on
Eyes. Lips. Ears. I thrash like a landed trout.
Utter silence. The world's noises are gone.

Frantic Flight, Rising, Rising

Maude was a goddess disguised as a small bird,
a budgie. Old John had no other family
since Mum had died. His childhood home gone. Absurd!

Grasping rellies stole his house, went on a spree,
took everything; John and Maude lived in a tent.
They planned to wreak their revenge on each trustee.

Because Maude was growing. She'd make them repent
then kill them quick, rip out their throats with her beak.
John would wrest back his home, and every last cent.

Maude grew to the size of a roc. Gorgeous freak!
John would ride tall on her back, fly high, hot-spurred
for his vengeance. But Maude grabbed him, gave a shriek,

and tore him apart. Dying, his vision blurred.
Maude was a goddess disguised as a small bird.

Galérien

They lash our backs, and boom the drum.
The timbers of our galley thrum
as missiles hit – will we succumb?

I haul my oar, sweat grimed, mind dull;
the other ship, propelled by scull
advances, rams, destroys our hull.

Our broken boards let in the sea.
We list and flood, brine covers me;
my shackles bite, I can't get free.

This ship of slaves is sinking down,
a dance of corpses all around.
And yet, I find I cannot drown?

Our ship hits bottom, splits its keel,
the fishes flock in frenzied zeal.
We oarsmen will become their meal.

Is every man the same as me?
Their bodies dead, subsumed by sea
but minds alive to some degree?

Upon the sandy ocean floor
the shrimps, and crabs, and beasts galore
start feasting on our wretched store.

They nibble at my hands and feet –
soon, leg consumed of all its meat
releases me from iron cleat.

I float towards the ocean's skin,
a blighted soul, a demon, djinn,
when shark bite tears my abdomen.

Gases leave my belly fast,
I start to sink again, aghast,
back down to mandibles I'm cast.

Now on the ocean floor I lay
as creatures gnaw my brains away.
When nothing's left, I'll die...I pray.

On the Cusp

Alone, she turns on the rooftop
and gazes out
at the city, afire by night,
the lights a gout

of colours. They clamour for heed.
No chance of rest
on high from chaos and clutter
either. Her quest

has reached its last dead end. A hope
for perspective
lost. She is just as small up here,
and fears to live.

The city lights would keep shining
without a stop.
Everything would remain in sight
if she might drop

into the ether. Looking down,
the pavements flow
with people intent on their goals,
souls who don't know

about her resolve... They'd be fine.
Thumbing their phones,
they'd upload for guaranteed likes
her spiked, rent bones...

Could morning bring a change of mind?
She turns again,
surveys the neon, shining bright,
fights for breath, then—

An Unusual Request

My husband had a stroke. He thinks he's dead
but eats bread and often drinks
while imagining he stinks
of decay. A custom-built coffin, please.
For his ease a mattress; in
the lid, air holes by his chin.
Tradesman, don't leave. Wait! *Oh, Tod?* Just pretend.
Look, dear, a friend. Yes, it's odd,
but I'll pay well. See? Cash wad!
How did Tod "die"? His hand held by a nurse,
which transferred the curse. She planned
to free herself from the damned.
Yes, so bizarre! Medical folk, perplexed,
feel vexed and guess it's the stroke
to blame. Just nod, don't provoke
him or he'll get upset and start to yell.
In a nutshell, we want art.
My sketch will give you a start.
What? Oh, Tod won't take meds. He feels his brain
is a withered bloodstain. Eels
of rot swim from head to heels.
You'll build his coffin? I'll pay top dollar.
No squalor in this house. Hey,
let's shake on the deal, okay?
Tod, grab his hand! Quick! Secure our release.
I want peace! Good. We'll procure
immunity now. We're sure
of freedom, but... Oh, you poor tradesman!
Onset does stun, there's no doubt,
but stops fast as a brownout.
Can you hear me? Tradesman? You'll be all right.
Sharp pains tonight will bite cruel,
then, voila... You'll be the ghoul.

The Door

All I have to do is open my fist
and let everything run from my hand.
When I close my eyes, I can sense the mist,
the welcoming dark, yet understand

that, maybe, others will be hurt if I
swap this empty cup of nothing left
for whatever comes next. More nothing? Sky
fairies? Homecoming? The warp and weft

of years bested me, eroded my will.
Some years wove small promises, but no,
cut the other way, bled me. Cut me still.
Life would play on if I failed to show.

Perhaps life might leave me first, deciding
that I don't deserve it anymore.
Then a lone spark could flare, overriding
this cut-off blackness that weights my core.

All I know is: I just don't know.
Lost, I count the days. One more. One more.
The world would turn, yes, if I were to go.
I clench my fist and long for the door.

The Coach from Castlemaine

In Castlemaine, the coaches lined the station at its heart
And the air smelled rank with dust and horses' sweat.
Minnie Sutton looked for porters, had a hold of luggage cart
While her little son named Edward seemed to fret.
"Can you see the coach we want?" cried Minnie, gazing
    down the row
As the noise and voices clamoured all about.
"It should stop at many towns but it will state that Bendigo
Is the final destination on the route."

They found the Cob & Co., the driver dropped down from his seat,
He was a thin and older man with scowling air,
And silently, he stowed their bags and didn't fuss to greet,
Minnie lifted Edward in, tried not to care.
A portly man of middle-age who held a fancy staff
Came aboard and dropped himself upon the bench.
"Good morning," Minnie said, the man let loose a hearty laugh
Replied, "The name is Pollard! Horseshit – what a stench!"

The driver, Blyth, secured the door and cracked the window pane,
Which helped to block the dust yet grant a breeze.
The carriage rocked, the horses neighed, the coach went
    down the lane
And the dandy showed his teeth and spread his knees.
"In Bendigo, I own a pub, I hope you'll not compete.
I can't afford to fight another foe."
But Minnie said, "We're selling clothes, a shop along the street,
And my husband hopes we'll have a win to show.

"We came from London," she explained, "in eighteen-sixty-one,
Yet our poultry farm just failed to thrive and died.
The foxes and the dingos took our stock despite the gun
And the fences, all the tricks and traps we tried."
The coach advanced, the buildings thinned, and Edward
    stared about

At the paddocks holding cattle, goats and sheep,
Then at eucalypts and mallee scrub, the stony land in drought
Until he yawned and laid on Minnie's lap to sleep.

They rode for miles through ironbark – a bugle sounding loud
Broke the quiet and started all of them awake.
"The changing station's coming up," the driver Blyth avowed,
"And, my fingers crossed, the missus offers cake."
At the home of logs and shingles, while the husband
    swapped the team,
His wife served up the stew and floury bun.
Then pulling Blyth aside, she gave her guests the
    cake and cream,
Millie overheard her say, "Have you a gun?"

"I store a rifle at my seat," he whispered, gave a curse,
"What's the news? Are thieves and robbers on the prowl?"
"A Yahoo-Devil-Devil," said the woman, "maybe worse,
Every farmer all around has heard its howl."
The driver scoffed and strode away. "That's superstitious lore."
Then he slapped the kitchen table with his hand.
"We have to leave at once if we're to reach the town by four."
And for not the first time, Minnie cursed the land.

Back on the coach while Edward drowsed, she crooked
    for Pollard's ear,
To ask, "What's 'Yahoo-Devil-Devil', pray?"
She figured it a dingo, but his answer gave her fear—
"Like the giant orang-utan from dark Malay.
Yet larger, more ferocious, hairy arms that reach the ground
And its instinct is to dash your brains from skull.
Some people call it *yowie*, 'round these parts it's quite renowned,
But I'm sure the truth in legend must be null."

In time, the rhythmic clopping of the horses' hooves did quell
All the passengers aboard into a doze.
Then the coach slammed to a halt and every horse began to yell,
And a wretched stink made Millie hold her nose.

"What the deuce?" said Pollard, angry, tapping cane
    upon the door
While Blyth exhorted *giddy-up* unto his team.
"If we're getting robbed by rangers," Pollard said, "I'll sue,
    for sure,
And I'll put this Cobb & Co. in low esteem."

Clinging hard to Minnie, Edward asked, "Are we to die?"
And the dread upon his face gave her some grit.
"It's nothing but a snake," she said, "that makes the horses shy."
Pollard spat, "A snake? My dear, you're full of shit."
She could see the huddled horses bunched on her side
    of the coach,
Rearing up with bulging eyes that showed the white,
There was something in the bushland, smelling rank,
    on the approach
And she gripped her little son who shook with fright.

A yard or two along the trail, the monster left the trees,
And Minnie's heart compressed at such a sight.
It was something of a giant, like the hairy chimpanzees
That they had viewed at London Zoo with such delight.
From underneath the bench she hauled out mailbag and a case
Urging, "Hide!" to Edward as she pushed him down.
"Stay there until I tell you," she said, packing in the space
While the horses shrieked in terror, pawed the ground.

The yowie ran and launched itself, the coach rocked on its bed,
And with Blyth in arms, the monster dropped to land.
Its yellowed fangs closed fast about the crown of his poor head
And the blood and gore of Blyth sprayed on the sand.
The monster slurped the brain up like an oyster from a spoon
Gently sucked at what remained as if at fruit.
Gagging, Minnie cried, "We need the rifle, quick, before I swoon,
It's at the driver's seat – and Pollard! I can shoot."

His face the hue of lard, he screamed and bolted from the coach
But instead of heading straight to get the gun,

Pollard, whimpering and sobbing at the yowie's quick approach,
Faced the wide and open bush, began to run.
The monster dropped the last of Blyth and jogged in hot pursuit
Like an ape, employing knuckles, swinging arms.
Minnie whispered to her son, "Stay there, I'm off to kill the brute
Then we'll ride the coach pell-mell and flee to farms."

She exited on shaking legs and groped towards the seat
Wrenching up her bustled skirt to climb aboard,
Her gut reaction – *take the reins!* – resulted in defeat
Since the frightened horses weren't of one accord.
The gun was one she knew, Martini-Henry, single shot
So, she packed the breech with cartridge, sighted in,
And here came Mister Pollard, purple suit a vivid blot
Against the bush – the yowie must have failed to win.

Minnie cried, "Did you escape?", but Pollard failed to shout,
So, she put her eye to rifle-sight and aimed.
And sure enough, his skull was gone, his face a bloodied gout
The yowie held him like a doll, one badly maimed.
She pulled the trigger – BANG – which stopped the yowie
    in its tracks
But the bullet hit the white of Pollard's shirt.
And cursing, Minnie fumbled with the bullets, spilled the packs,
While the yowie snarled, threw Pollard to the dirt.

"Mother, here!" came timid voice, 'twas Edward by her side,
With a cartridge in his hand, face wet with tears.
Yet she had no time to scold him, for the yowie took to stride
And she loaded up the gun, heart choked by fears.
She shot again and hit its arm, which didn't slow its pace
Yet it bellowed, loud and deep, such like a bear.
The bullet next punched hard into the dark hide of its face
And the yowie staggered, blood dripped down its hair.

She turned to Edward. "Take the gun!" she yelped, and
    took the rein
As the monster found its feet and tried to run.

But this time "Giddy up!" provoked the horses, and the train
Took off fast along the track – she cried, "Hold on!"
The messy gallop tossed the coach, which nearly took a spill
And the horses screeched and screamed in mortal fear,
For the yowie bounded fast upon their wake, was gaining still
Minnie said to Edward, "Do your best to steer."

The little boy took hold the straps, his mother took the gun
Resting barrel on the coach and taking aim,
And she thought of husband waiting for them, standing
    in the sun
Waiting for a coach that somehow never came.
The tremble in her fingers went away, she took a breath
Staring at the monster square within her sight,
And she pulled the trigger, sent the yowie straight unto its death.
As it dropped onto its face, she felt delight.

"Did you get it?" Edward said, as Minnie sat and took the reins.
He was rigid in his seat and couldn't scout.
"I got it and we're safe," she said, "I'm sure I'll find the lanes,
And we'll reach the town of Bendigo, no doubt."
Edward sobbed and sagged against her; they were all
    atremble still
But after time the rattled horses settled down,
And the coach from Castlemaine at last descended final hill
Spread before them, Bendigo, the promised town.

Wheals and Whorls

Here's an anecdote
from my youth: a boat
motors through surf, out
to view the seals.

I'm sky-high on dope,
see the waves, their slope
through a microscope,
notice the wheals

and whorls of my skin
magnified therein—
realise all is twinned.
One universe.

Here's an anecdote
from old age: devote
all to ailments, dote
with drugs, a nurse.

On my hands the waves
roll, skin misbehaves
and seals peep from caves.
Nurse says it's hives.

This isn't a rash.
The seals stare and splash,
they stay though I slash
and cut with knives.

Afterword

Not everyone who enjoys poetry wants to peek behind the curtains, but if you like to discover how a poem is put together, the following will offer brief insights.

The Broonie
Inspiration: my flash fiction piece *"Post Hoc Ergo Propter Hoc"*

The villanelle originated in 17th-century France. Typically, the villanelle comprises 19 lines, consisting of five three-line stanzas (tercets) and one four-line stanza (quatrain). There are eight to 11 syllables per line, so I split the difference and chose 10. The rhyme scheme is ABA for the tercets and ABAA for the quatrain. The villanelle has only two repeating rhymes, and must include two repeating lines (refrains). With all these rules, it's no wonder the villanelle is known as 'exquisite torture'. Perhaps this is one of the reasons why "The Broonie" was shortlisted for an Australian Shadows 'Best Poem' Award.

Flamingo-Pink Balloon
Inspiration: my short story "A Faithful Companion"

The strambotto dates from 13th-century Italy. There are variations, but I selected the form with 11 syllables per line and eight lines per stanza. Instead of the typical rhyme scheme of ABABABAB, however, I played around and used ABABCDCD.

408 Kilometres Up
Inspiration: my flash fiction piece "Shedding"

The terzanelle is a mix of two poetic forms: the villanelle and the terza rima. It's 19 lines, comprising five tercets and a quatrain. The second line of each tercet must be repeated in the third line of the next stanza. To complicate matters further, the second and fourth lines of the quatrain must repeat the first and third lines of the first stanza. In all, seven lines are repeated.

Amazon Warrior
Inspiration: my short story "In the Company of Women"
   The Spanish décima espinela is typically 10 lines per stanza and eight syllables per line, with a rhyming scheme of ABBAACCDDC. Strictly speaking, the poem in its entirety is a single stanza, but I kept it going over 11 stanzas to write an 'epic' poem; a longer narrative typically used to describe the adventures of a hero.

First and Last Foray
Inspiration: my short story "Paramour"
   The Spanish quintain known as the flamenca is five lines per stanza, but you can combine the third and fourth lines into a single line to make a quatrain, which is what I did. To further help the narrative flow, I converted my 12 quatrains into six eight-line stanzas (octets).

The Sea Will Have
Inspiration: my short story "What the Sea Wants"
   The sonnet has 14 lines with 10 syllables per line. The Shakespearean sonnet, my inspiration here, has three quatrains and a finishing couplet of two rhyming lines. The couplet is meant to form the 'mic drop' of the poem by catching the reader off-guard with a startling or unexpected end.

Witchcraft Doll
Inspiration: my drabble "Talisman"
   The Irish poetic form cethramtu rannaigechta moire comprises quatrains with only three syllables per line. The second and third lines of each quatrain must rhyme.

Ancient Cogs Beneath
Inspiration: my short story "The Sand"
   The three-quatrain chain has 12 lines. The lines are meant to interlock, with the last word or syllable of each line forming the first word or syllable of the next. The rhyming scheme is XAXA XBXB XCXC, with X being unrhymed.

The Midwife
Inspiration: my short story "Will o' the wisp"
    The ballad is a narrative story told in four-line stanzas, with the second and fourth line of each stanza rhyming. I chose 14 syllables for lines one and three, and 11 syllables for lines two and four, to mimic the bush-ballad style of Australian poetic legend Banjo Paterson.

Into My Parlour
Inspiration: my flash fiction piece "Fortune teller"
    The French dizain originated in the 15th century, and consists of 10 lines with 10 syllables per line. The rhyme scheme is ABABBCCDCD, meaning the pattern of the verse's second half is the mirror image of the first.

Sarah Joins the Circus
Inspiration: my flash fiction piece "Sarah Jane Runs Away with the Circus"
    The Welsh poetic form gwawdodyn byr uses quatrains. In each quatrain, the first two lines consist of nine syllables each, with 10 syllables each in the last two lines. Lines one, two and four rhyme at the end. Interestingly, a word somewhere around the middle of line three must also rhyme with the same sound.

Parasitic Births
Inspiration: my short story "Hair and Teeth"
    The French rondeau dates from medieval times. Its 15 lines comprise three verses: a five-line stanza (quintet), a quatrain, and a six-line stanza (sestet). The rhyme scheme is AABBA AABR AABBAR, with R being a repeated line (refrain).

Smothered, Still and Silent
Inspiration: my short story "Angel Hair"
    The French ballade is 28 lines, comprising three eight-line stanzas and a quatrain. The last line of each stanza is a refrain (R). Each line can be eight or 10 syllables; I chose 10. The rhyme scheme is ABABBCBR ABABBCBR ABABBCBR BCBR.

Frantic Flight, Rising, Rising
Inspiration: my short story "The Littlest Avian"

The closed terza rima sonnet combines elements of the terzanelle and the terza rima. While there are variations, it's basically a 14-line poem comprising four tercets and a couplet. The rhyme scheme I chose is ABA BCB CDC DAD AA, with the first and last lines of the poem being the same.

Galérien
Inspiration: my flash fiction piece "Cast down"

The triplet is a type of tercet, or three-line stanza, but all three lines of each stanza must rhyme. Therefore, the rhyme scheme is AAA BBB CCC and so on. Every line has the same number of syllables. Most sources consider that the number of syllables is up to the poet; I chose eight, a number which is commonly used across many forms of poetry.

On the Cusp
Inspiration: my flash fiction piece "Rooftop"

The Irish form dechnad cummaisc uses quatrains with two differing line lengths. The first and third lines are eight syllables, while the second and fourth lines comprise four syllables that rhyme at the end. To complicate matters, the last word in the third line must also rhyme or assonate (have a similar sound) with a word somewhere in the middle of the fourth line.

An Unusual Request
Inspiration: my short story "Delirium of Negation"

The Welsh englyn penfyr is built around the tercet. The first line of each tercet comprises 10 syllables, while the second and third lines have seven syllables each. The first line has a word somewhere within that must rhyme with the end syllable of the second and third lines. Also, the last syllable of the first line must assonate or rhyme with a word in the second line. For the sake of story flow, I ran all the tercets together.

The Door
Inspiration: my short story "Molly, Dearest Molly"
The decasyllabic quatrain comprises stanzas of four lines with each line having 10 syllables. The rhyme scheme is ABAB. This is an unusual poem for my collection because it doesn't reference in any way the plot of the story upon which it's based; rather, it tries to capture the mood and melancholy of the POV character instead.

The Coach from Castlemaine
Inspiration: my short story "Stagecoach from Castlemaine"
Similar to my poem "The Midwife", I used a bush-ballad form. This is my homage to the rhythm used by Banjo Paterson in such Australian classics as "The Man from Snowy River".

Wheals and Whorls
Inspiration: my drabble "Sealskin"
The Welsh cyhydedd hir consists of quatrains. The first, second and third line of each quatrain comprise five syllables, and rhyme at the end. The fourth line is four syllables. In a set of two quatrains, the fourth line of the first quatrain rhymes with the fourth line of the second quatrain.

When I decided to venture into poetry, I set myself the task of writing in a variety of different poetic forms. Achieving this has been both challenging and immensely satisfying.

First Publication Credits

Poems are original to this collection unless listed below.

"The Broonie" *Nightmare Fuel magazine*, 2023

"Flamingo-Pink Balloon" *Trembling with Fear*, The Horror Tree, 2022

"408 Kilometres Up" *AntipodeanSF #287*, 2022

Amazon Warrior – *Illumen Magazine Autumn 2023*, Hiraeth Publishing, 2023

The Sea Will Have – *AntipodeanSF #257*, 2020

Witchcraft Doll – *Nightmare Fuel magazine*, 2022

The Midwife – *Nightmare Fuel Magazine*, 2023

Parasitic Births – *Nightmare Fuel magazine*, 2022

Smothered, Still and Silent – *Midnight Echo #17*, 2022

Galérien – *Illumen Magazine Summer 2024*, Hiraeth Publishing, 2024

An Unusual Request – *Penumbric Speculative Fiction Magazine*, 2025

The Coach from Castlemaine – *Liminal Spaces: Horror Stories* by Deborah Sheldon, IFWG Publishing, 2022

Wheals and Whorls – *Illumen Magazine Winter 2023*, Hiraeth Publishing, 2023

Author Biography

DEBORAH SHELDON is a multi-award-winning author and anthology editor from Melbourne, Australia. She writes poems, short stories, novellas and novels across the darker spectrum of horror, crime and noir. Her award-nominated titles include the novels *Cretaceous Canyon*, *Body Farm Z*, *Contrition*, and *Devil Dragon*; the novella *Thylacines*; and collections *Figments and Fragments: Dark Stories*, and *Liminal Spaces: Horror Stories*. Her latest releases include the novel *Bodily Harm*, and her anthology *Spawn 2: More Weird Horror Tales About Pregnancy, Birth and Babies*.

Deb's collection *Perfect Little Stitches and Other Stories* won the Australian Shadows 'Best Collected Work' Award, was shortlisted for an Aurealis Award, and long-listed for a Bram Stoker. Her short fiction has been widely published, shortlisted for numerous Australian Shadows and Aurealis Awards, translated, and included in various 'best of' anthologies.

Her poetry has been published in various magazines including *Illumen*, *Nightmare Fuel* and *Midnight Echo*. Her poem "The Broonie" was shortlisted for the Australian Shadows 'Best Poem' Award.

Deb has won the Australian Shadows 'Best Edited Work' Award three times: for *Midnight Echo 14*, and for the anthologies she conceived and edited, *Spawn: Weird Horror Tales About Pregnancy, Birth and Babies*, and *Killer Creatures Down Under: Horror Stories with Bite*. As a senior editor at IFWG Publishing, she specialises in horror anthologies.

Other credits include feature articles for magazines, non-fiction books (Reed Books, Random House), TV scripts such as NEIGHBOURS, stage and radio plays, and award-winning medical writing. Visit Deb at http://deborahsheldon.wordpress.com

www.ingramcontent.com/pod-product-compliance
Lightning Source LLC
LaVergne TN
LVHW081456060526
838201LV00051BA/1814